ZOOM! ZOOM!

written by **LOLA M. SCHAEFER**
illustrated by **KIRK PARRISH**

Ready-to-Read

Simon Spotlight
New York London Toronto Sydney New Delhi

Here is a list of all the words you will find in this book. Sound them out before you begin reading the story.

Names:

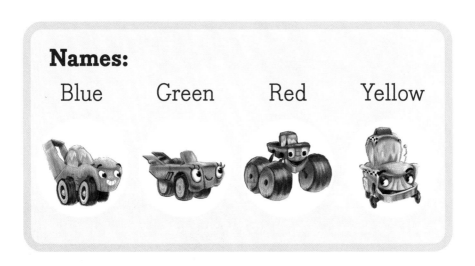

Blue   Green   Red   Yellow

SIMON SPOTLIGHT
An imprint of Simon & Schuster Children's Publishing Division
1230 Avenue of the Americas, New York, New York 10020
This Simon Spotlight edition May 2024
Text copyright © 2024 by Lola M. Schaefer
Illustrations copyright © 2024 by Kirk Parrish
All rights reserved, including the right of reproduction in whole or in part in any form.
SIMON SPOTLIGHT, READY-TO-READ, and colophon are registered trademarks of Simon & Schuster, LLC.
Simon & Schuster: Celebrating 100 Years of Publishing in 2024
For information about special discounts for bulk purchases, please contact Simon & Schuster Special Sales at
1-866-506-1949 or business@simonandschuster.com.
Manufactured in the United States of America 0324 LAK
2 4 6 8 10 9 7 5 3 1
CIP data for this book is available from the Library of Congress.
ISBN 978-1-6659-5170-8 (hc)
ISBN 978-1-6659-5169-2 (pbk)
ISBN 978-1-6659-5171-5 (ebook)

Word families:

"-ace" ⟶ place   race

"-ast" ⟶ fast   last   past

"-in" ⟶ grin   in   spin   win

Sight words:

all	and	go	goes	is
no	one	that	three	to
two	what			

Bonus words:

bang	cars	more	oh
pulls	round	slow	stops
wants	zoom	zooms	

Ready to go? Happy reading!

Don't miss the questions about the story
on the last page of this book.

Zoom! Zoom!
Blue wants to race.
Blue is in place.

Three, two, one, GO!
Go, Blue, go!

Oh no!

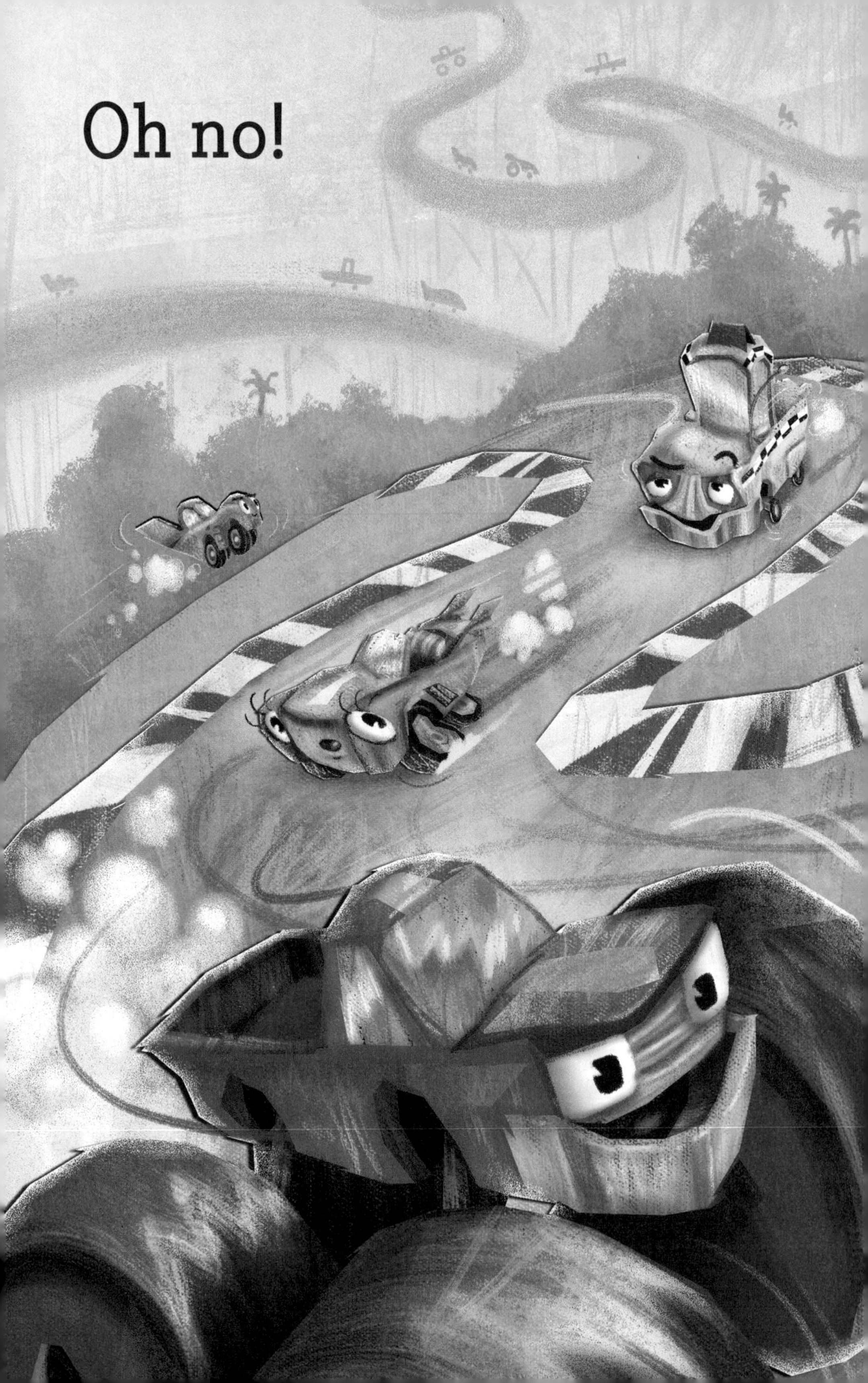

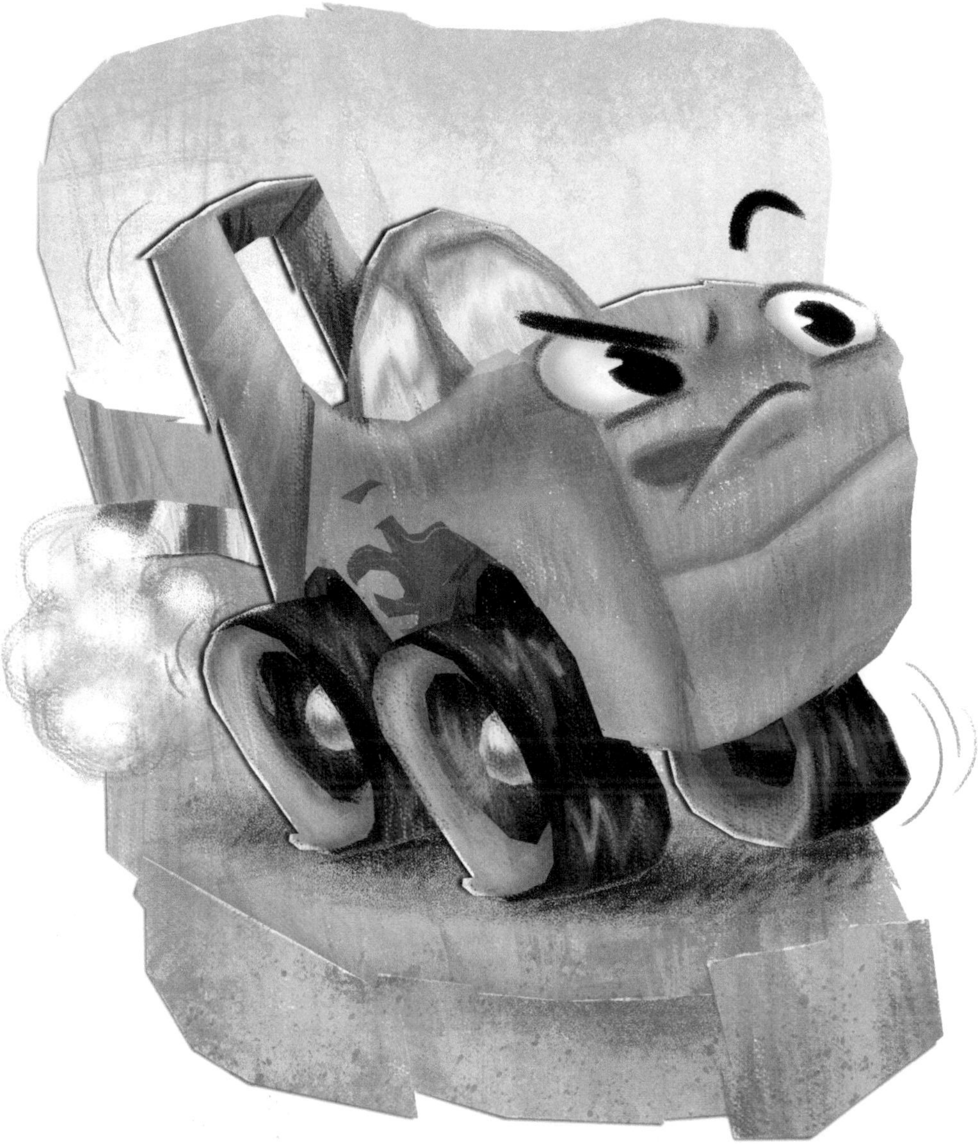

Blue goes slow.

Blue is last!

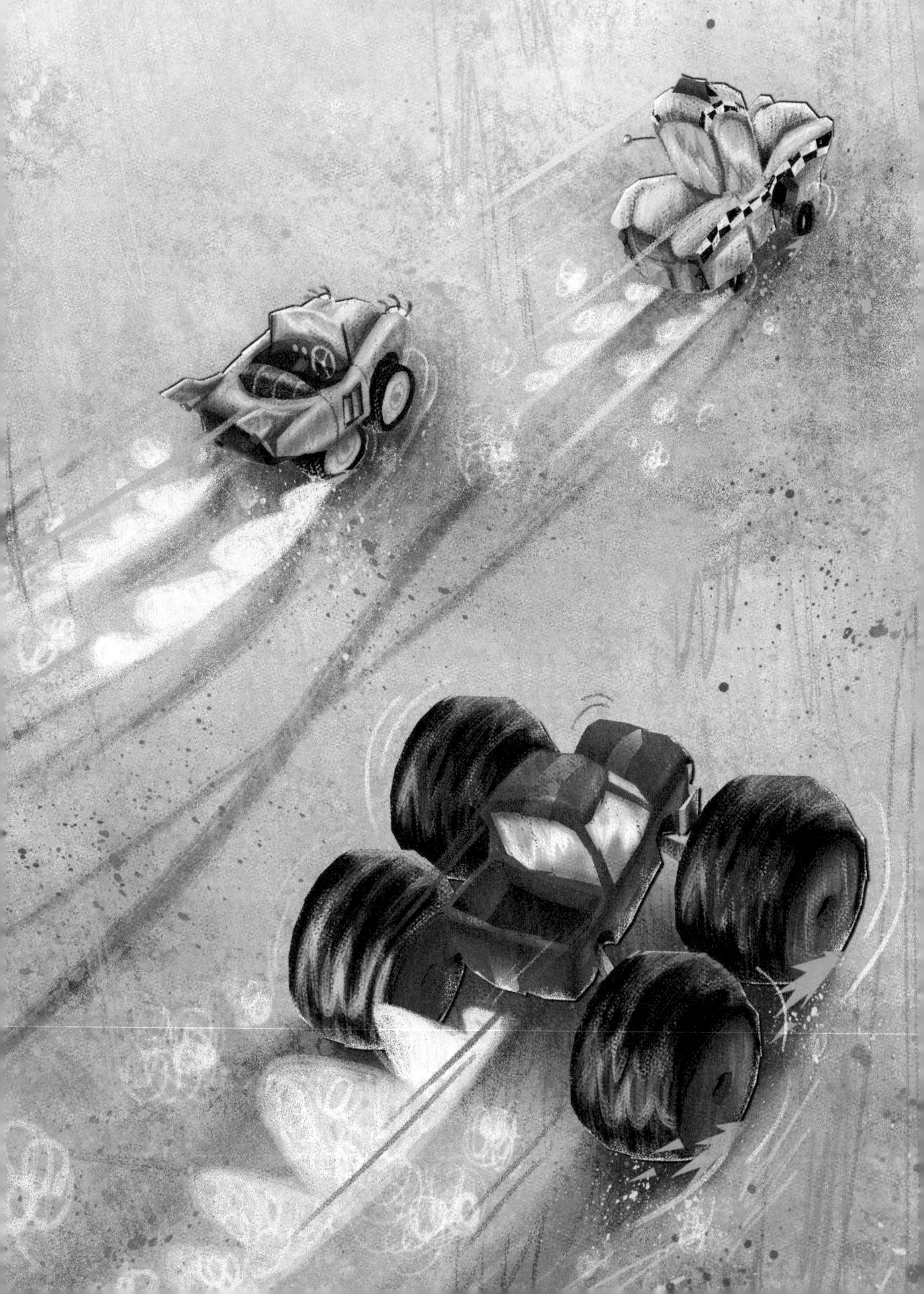

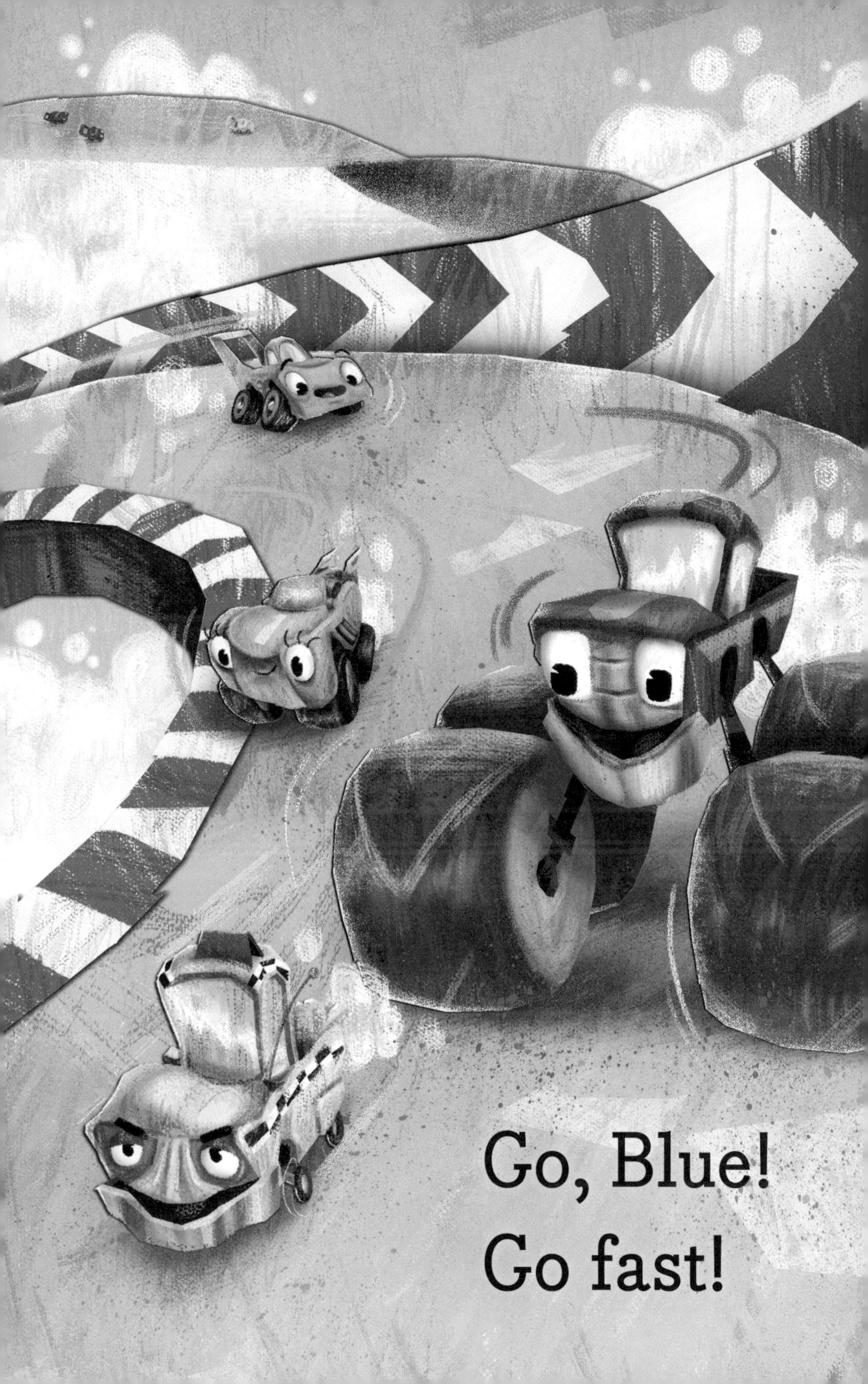

Go, Blue!
Go fast!

Zoom! Zoom!
Blue goes fast.

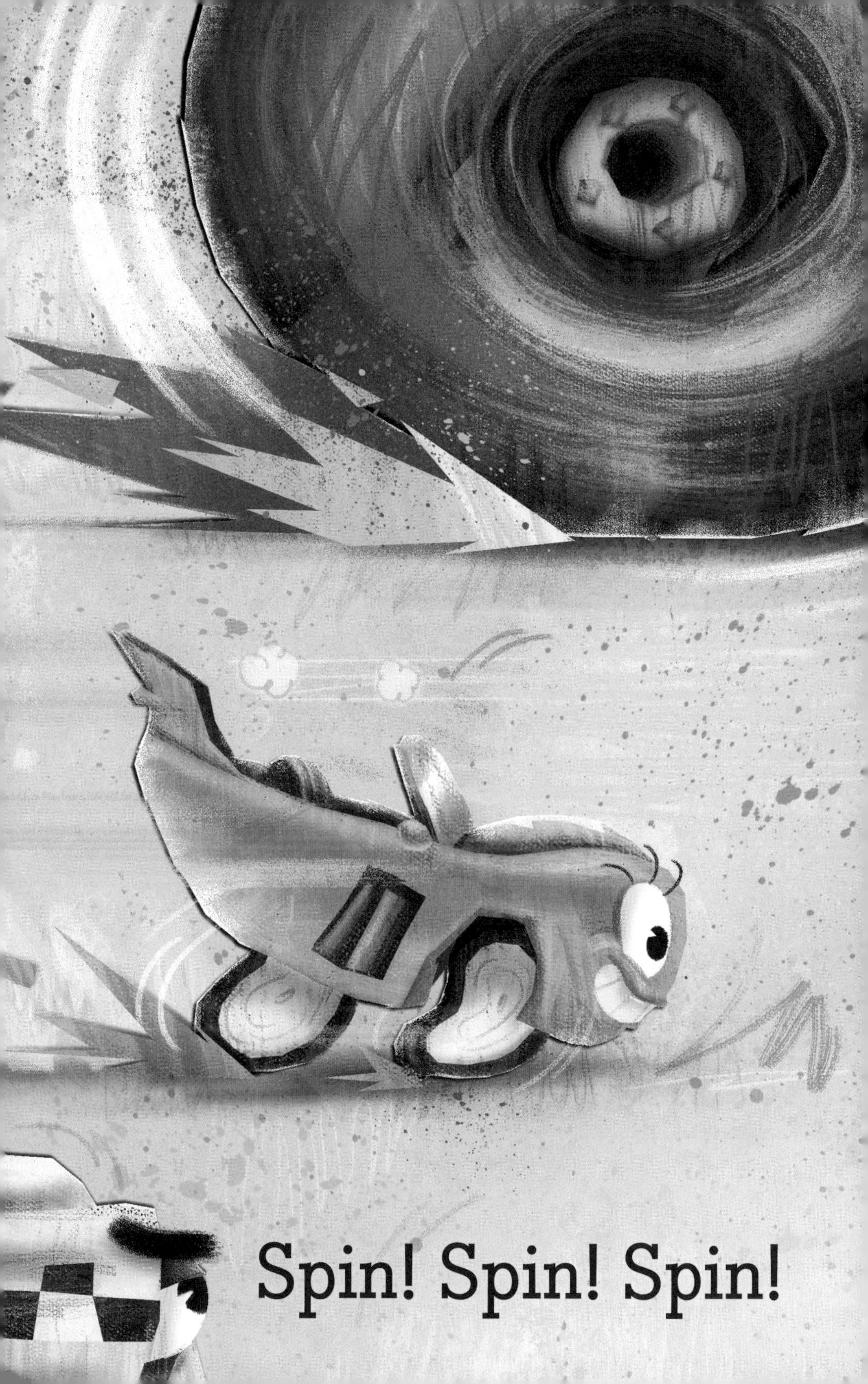

Spin! Spin! Spin!

Blue zooms
past Red,

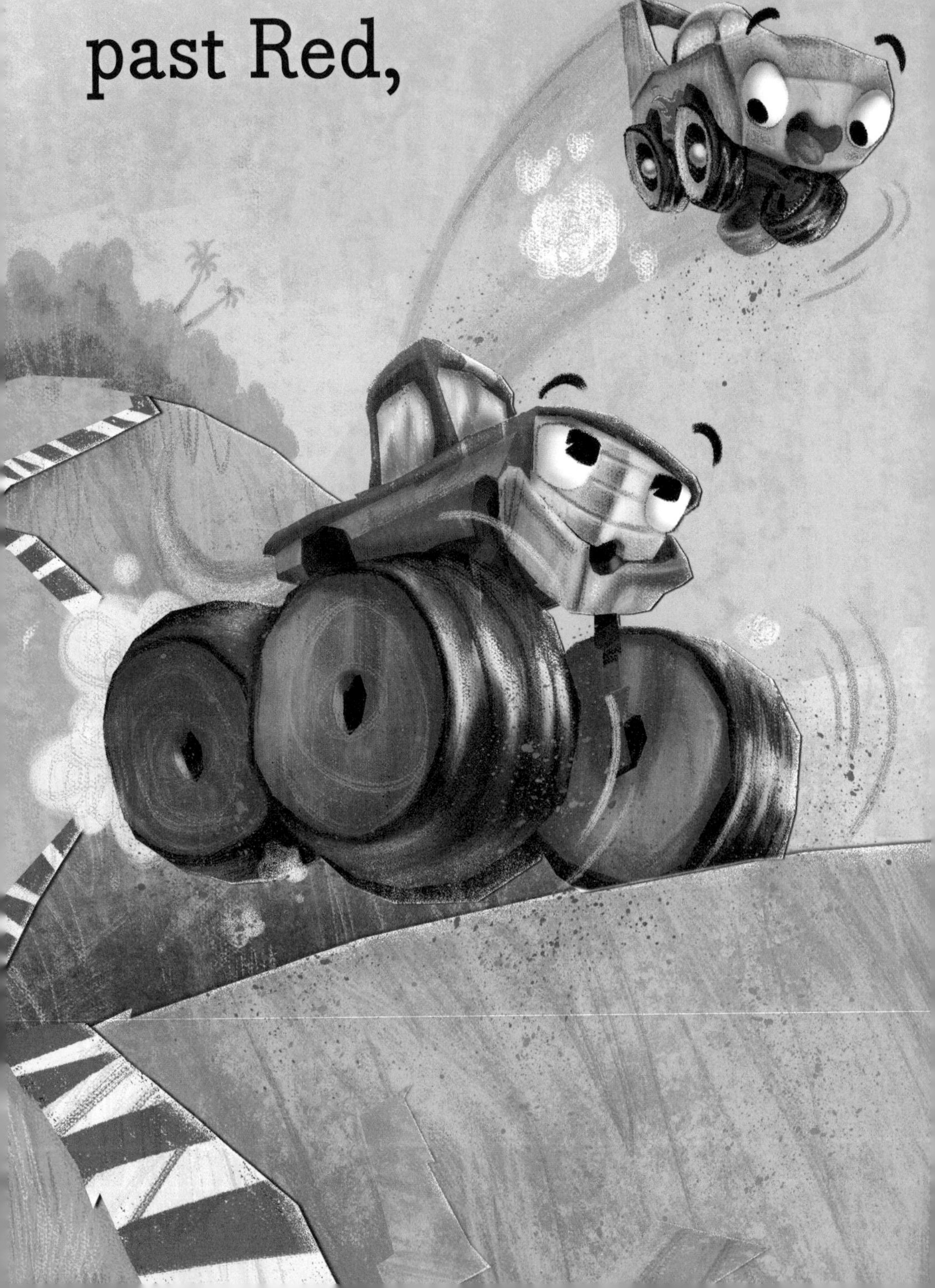

past Yellow,
and past Green.

Zoom! Zoom!

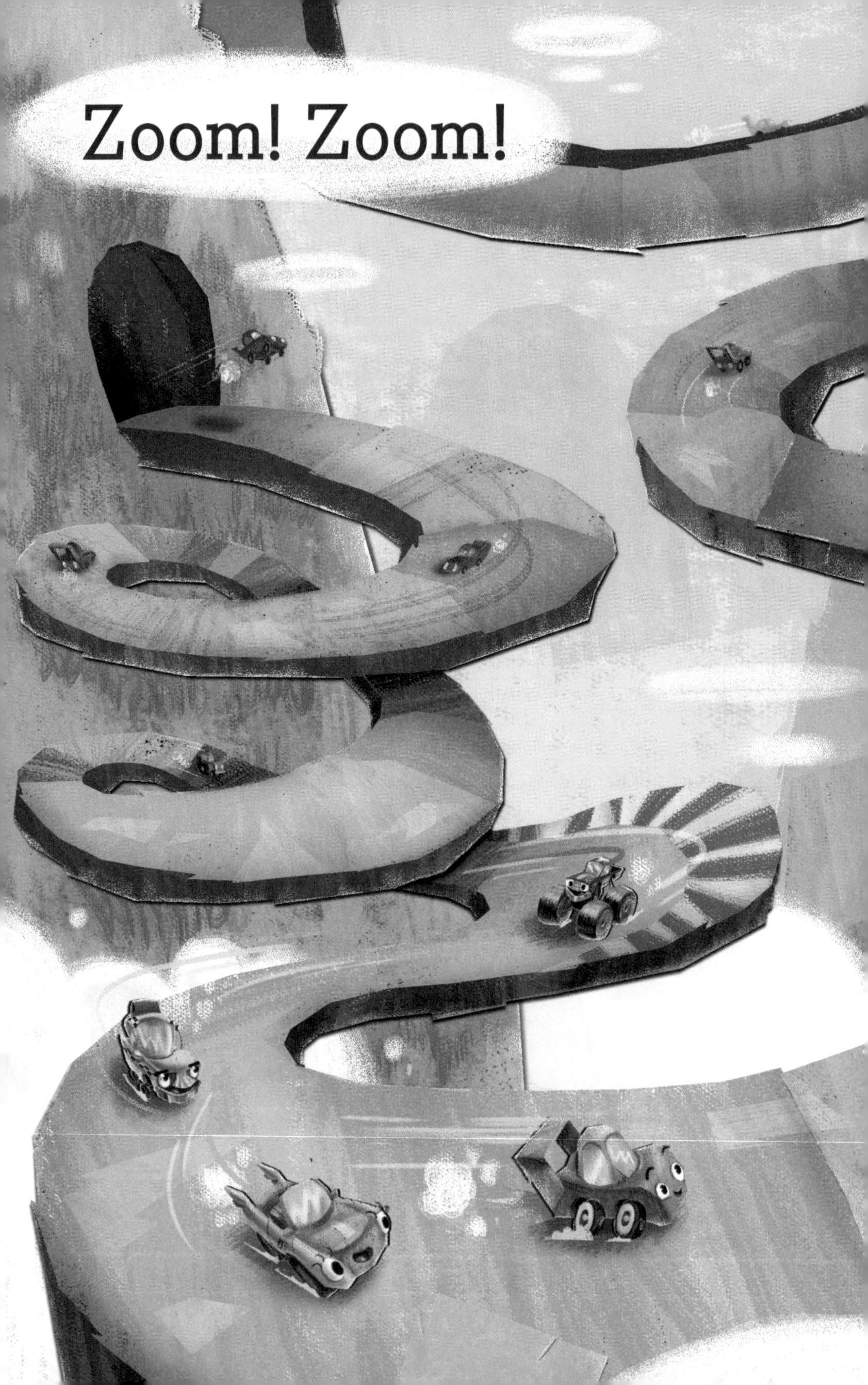

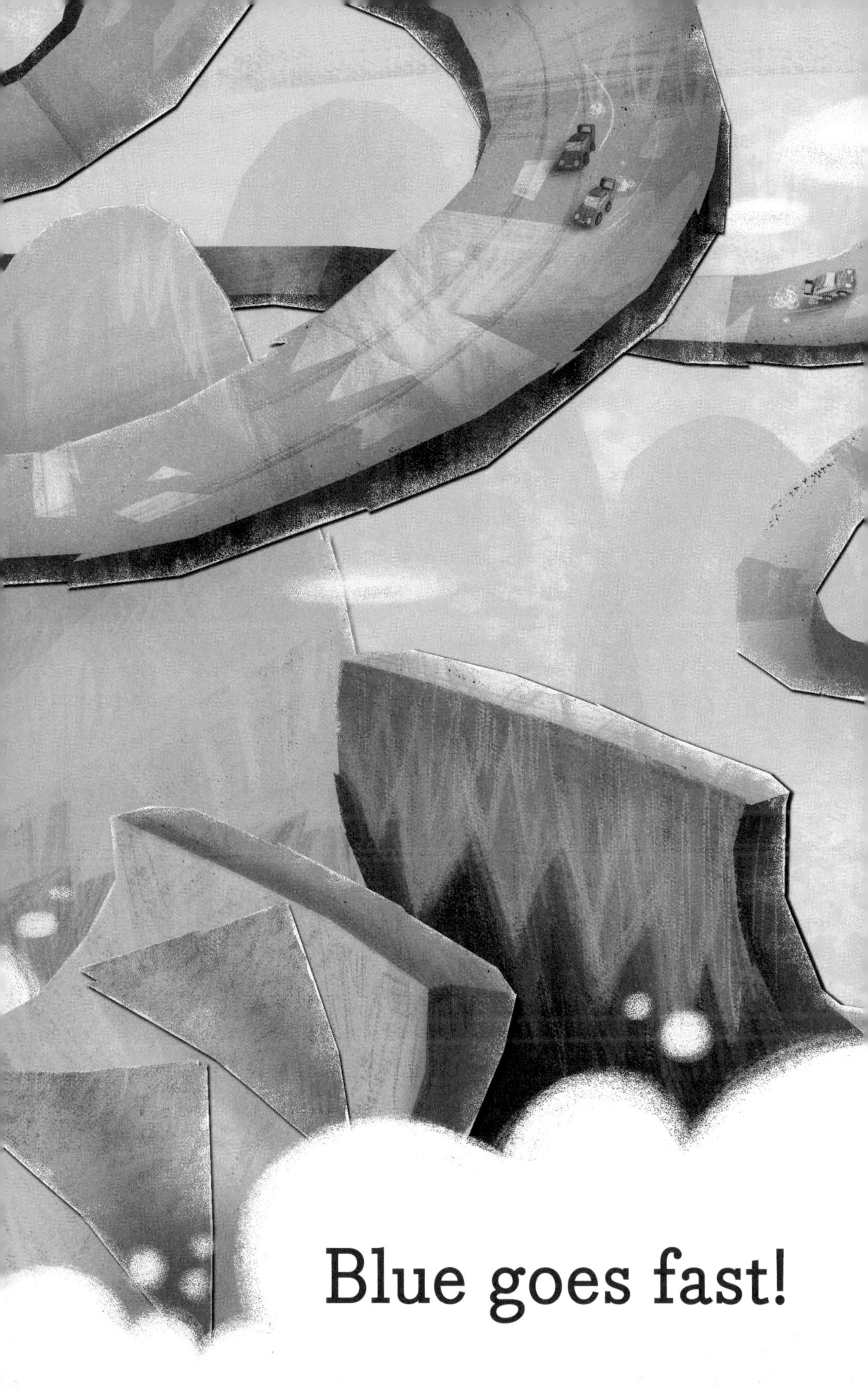

Blue goes fast!

Oh no!
What is that?

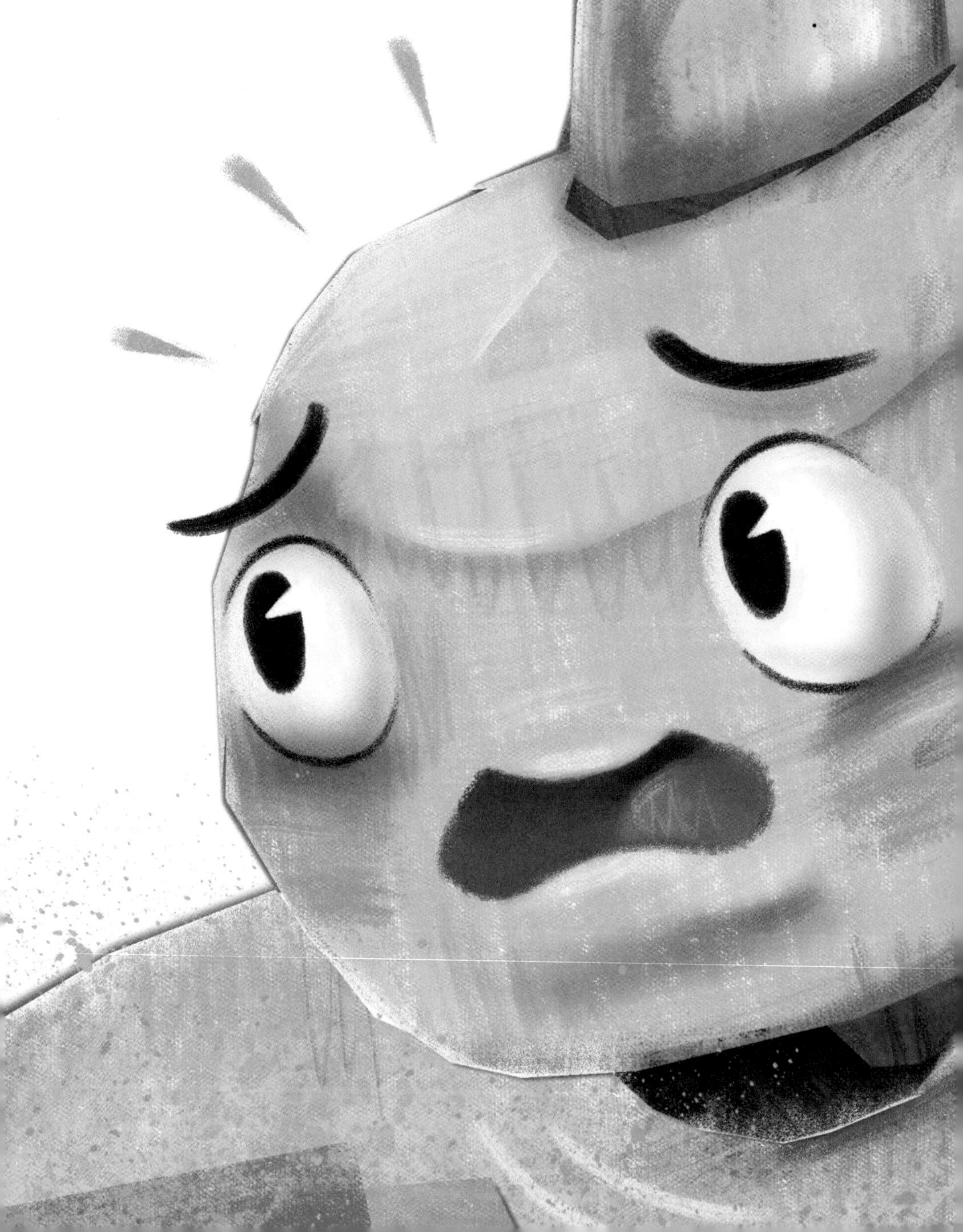

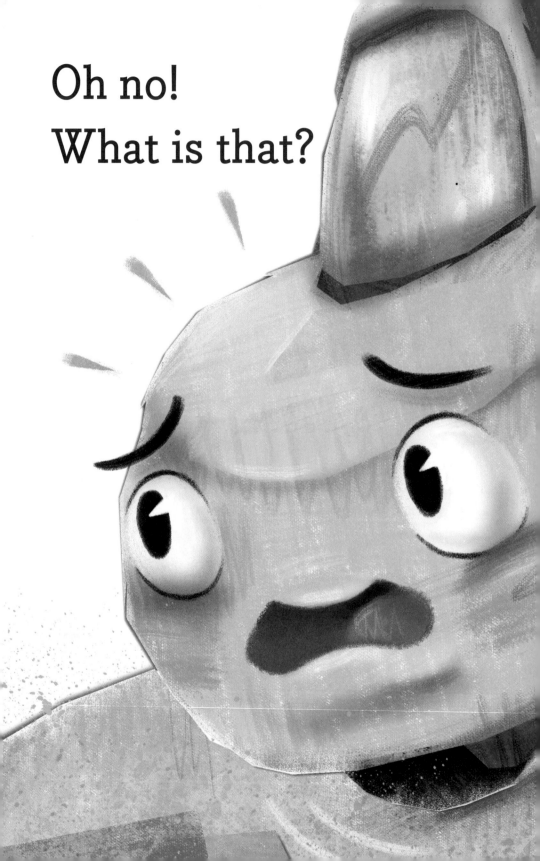

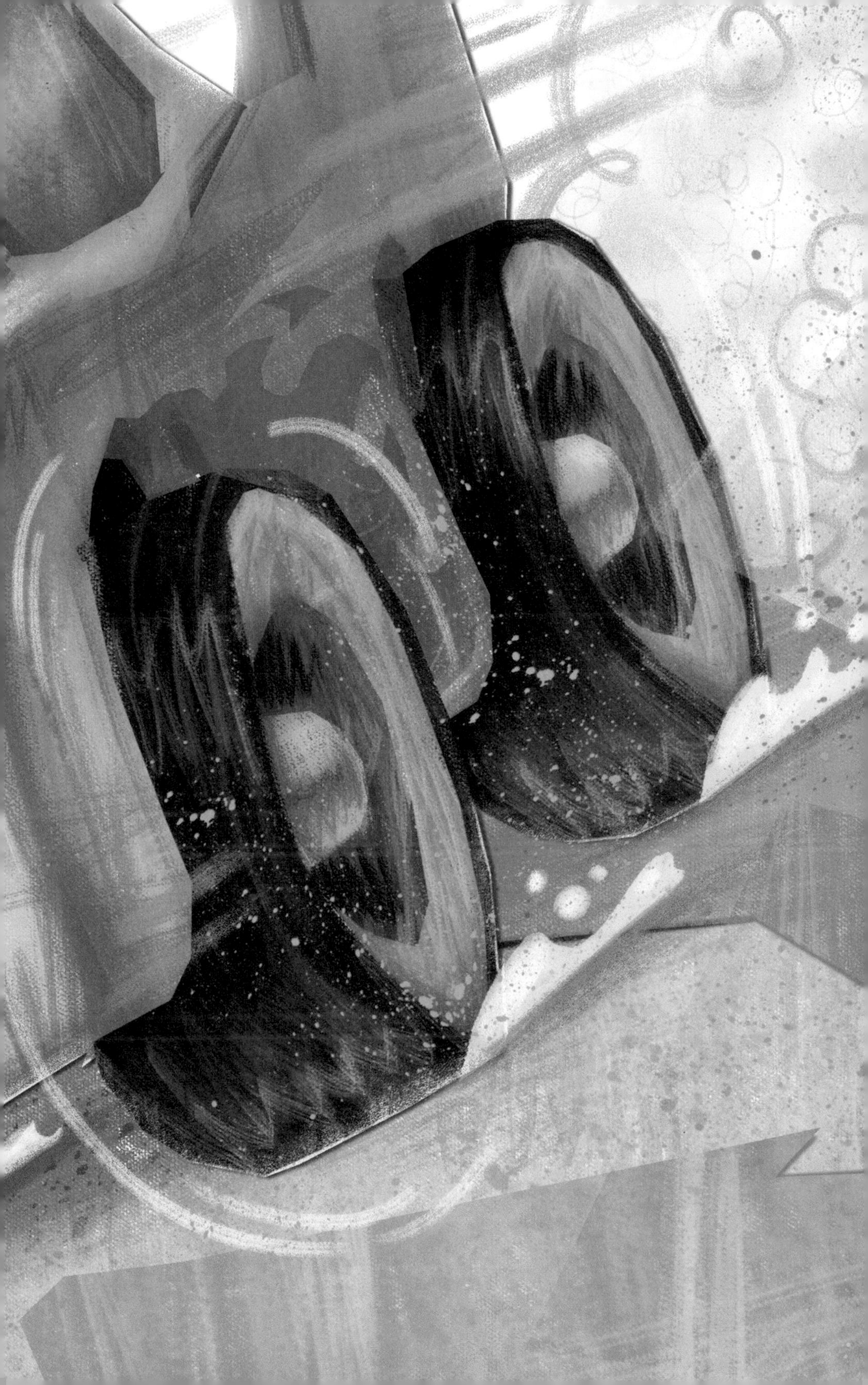

Spin! Spin! Spin!

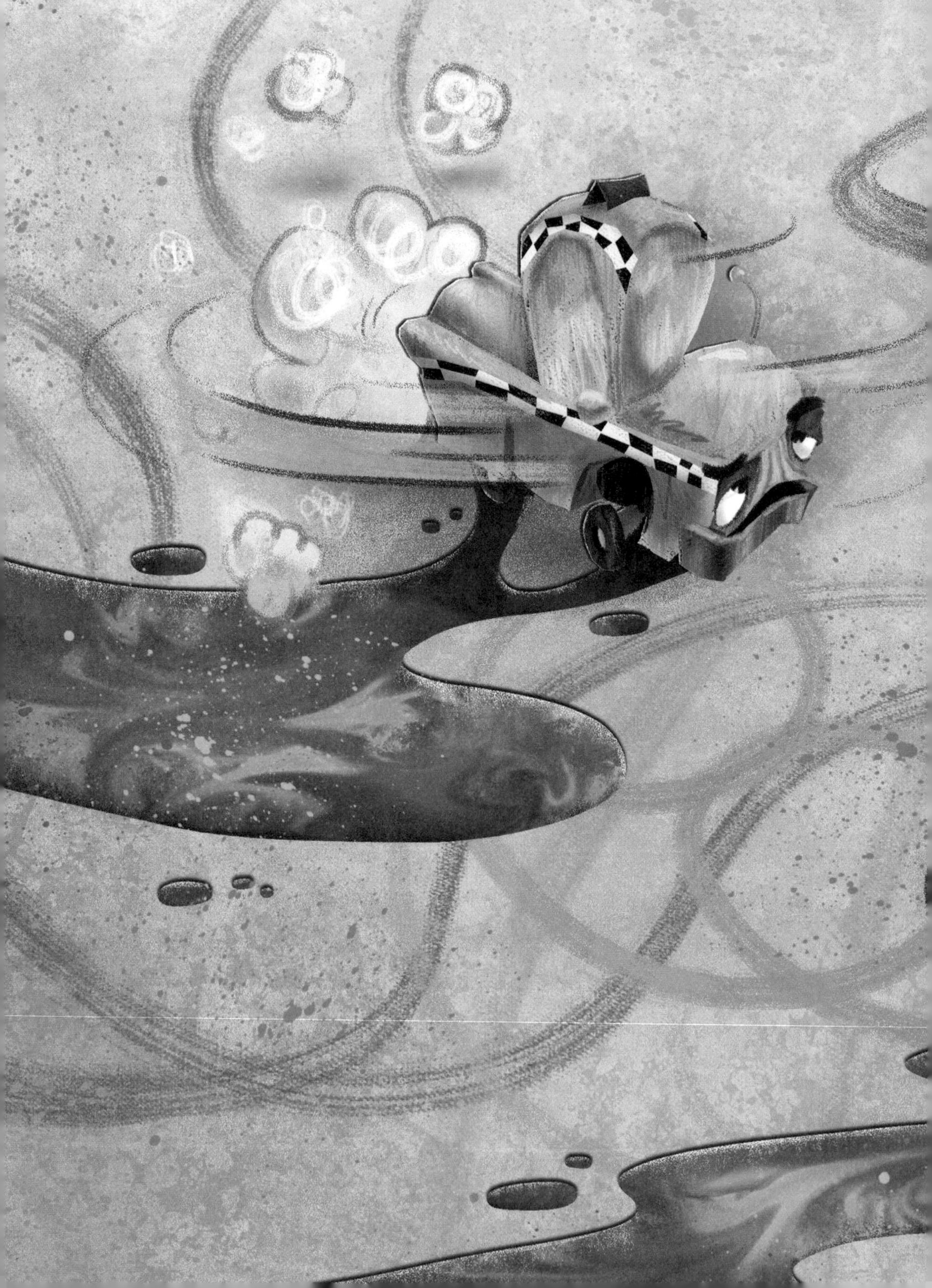

Round and round and round.

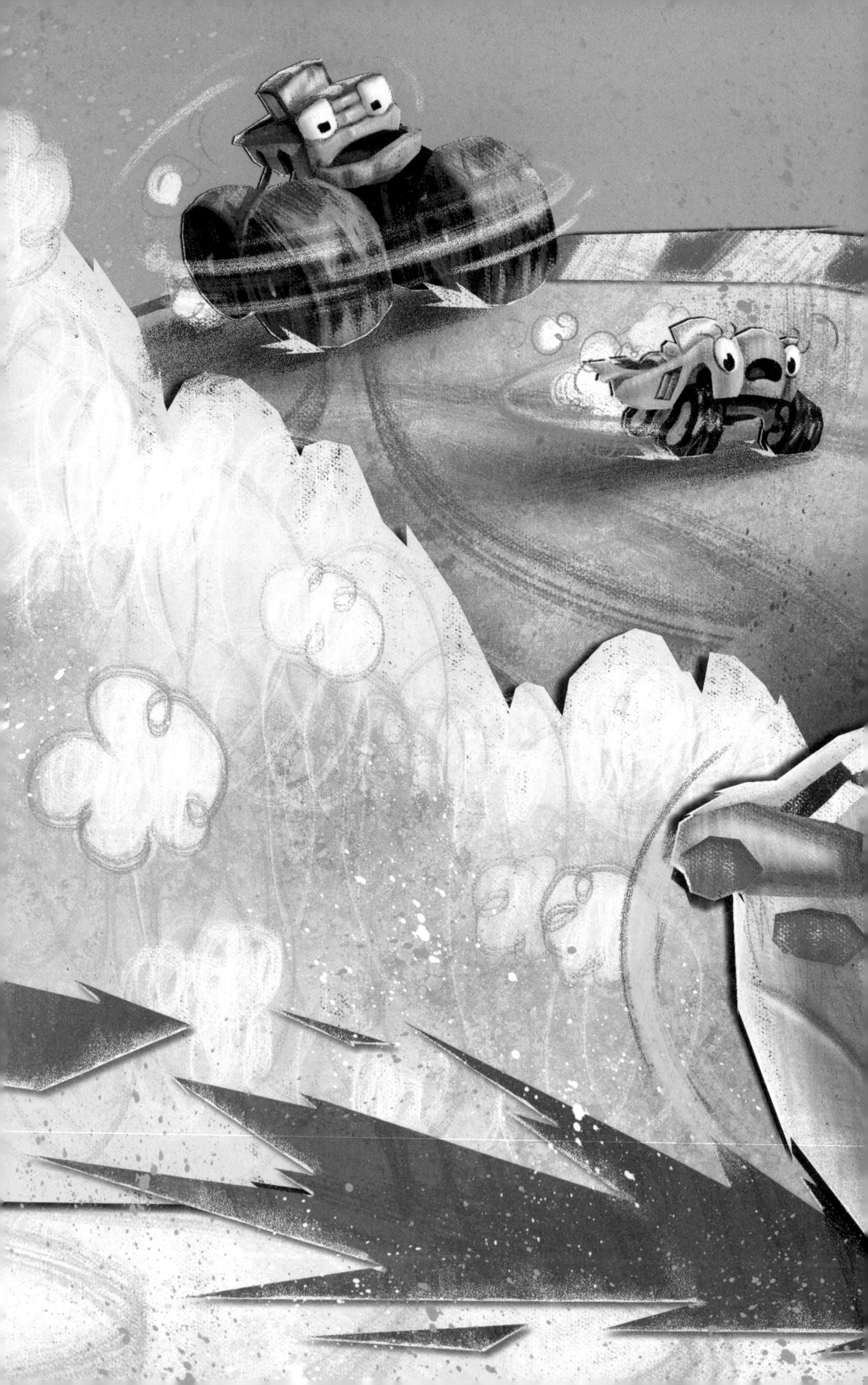

BANG!

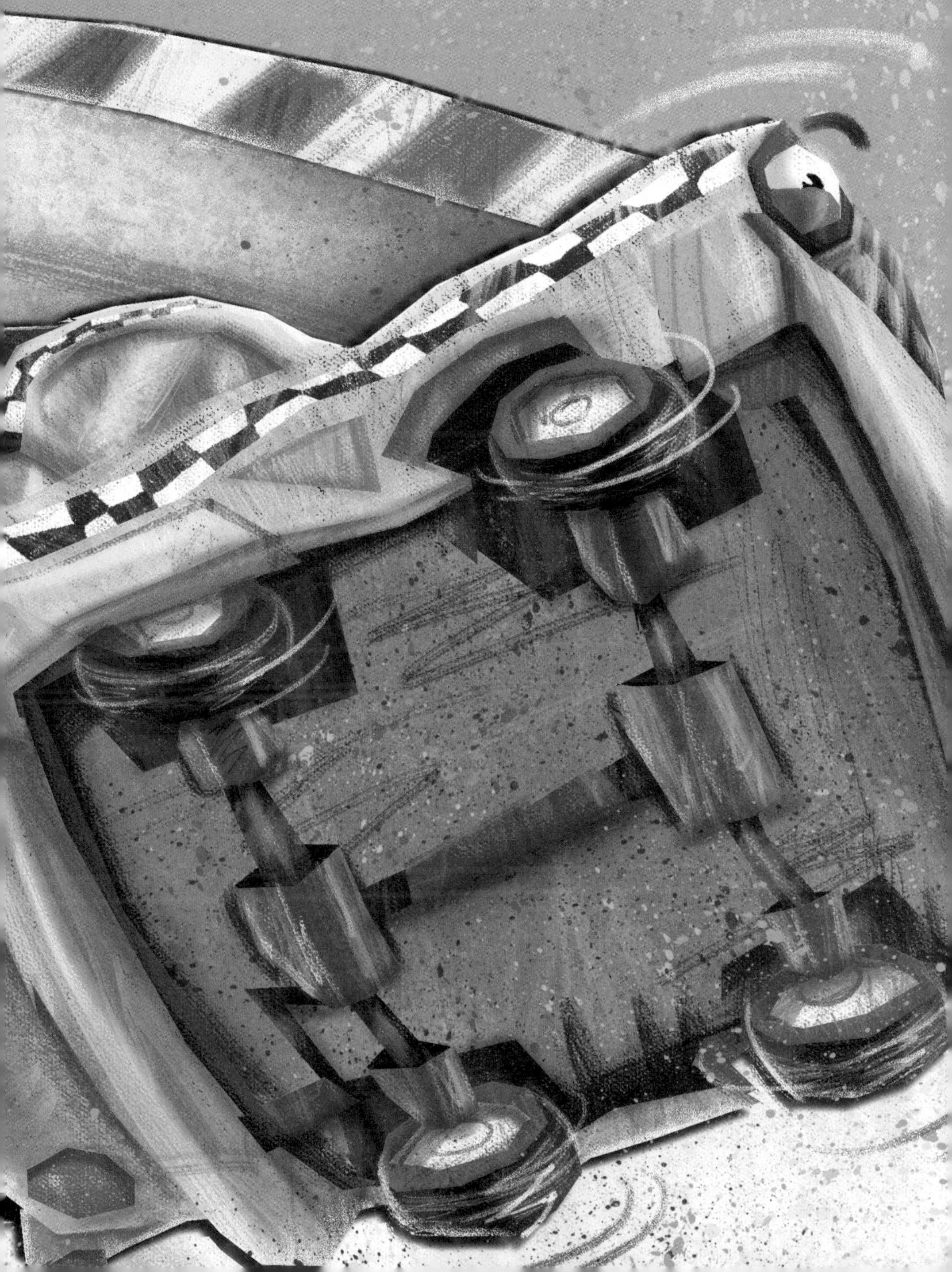

Red stops.

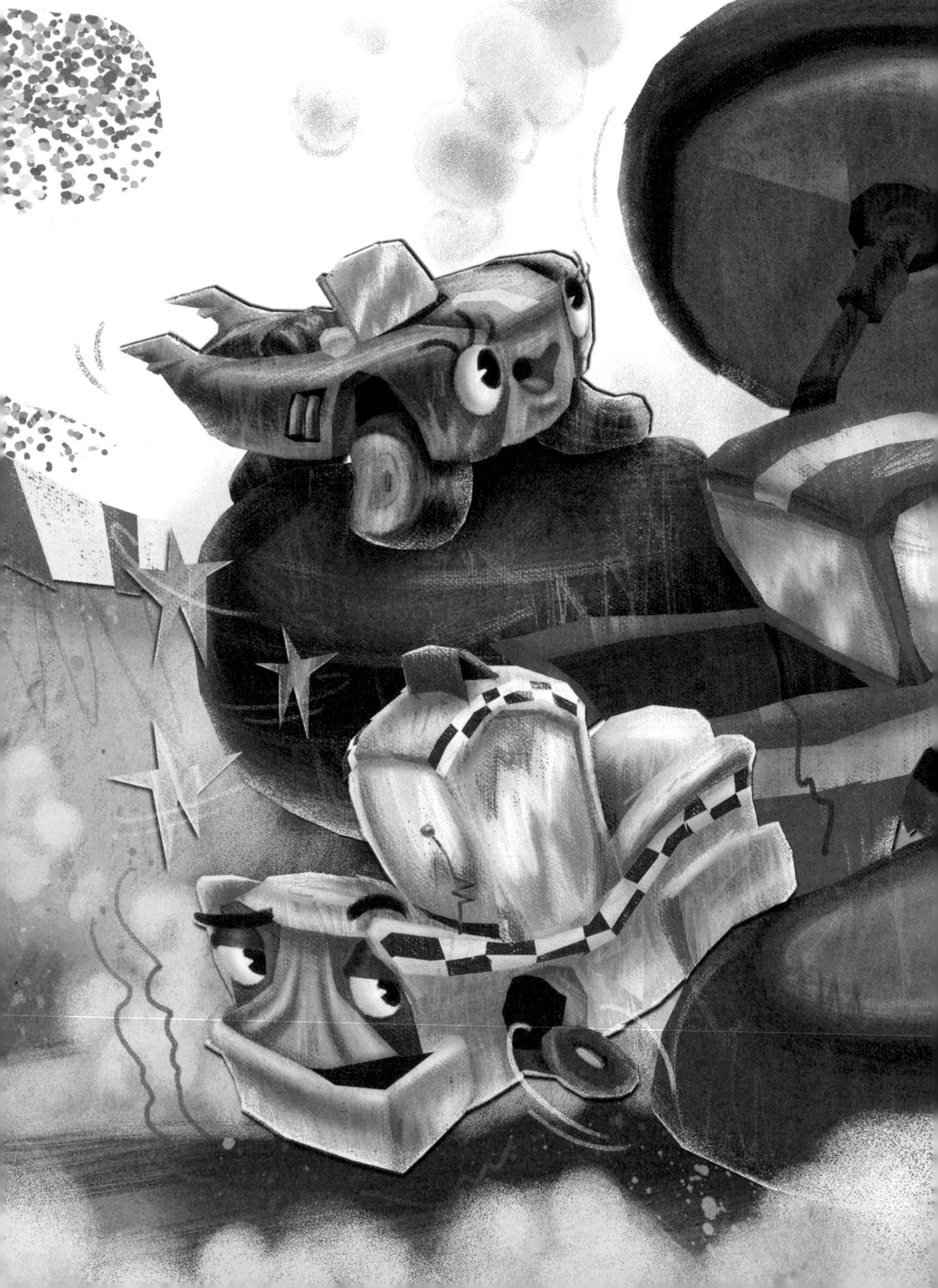

Yellow stops.

Green stops.

Blue goes slow.

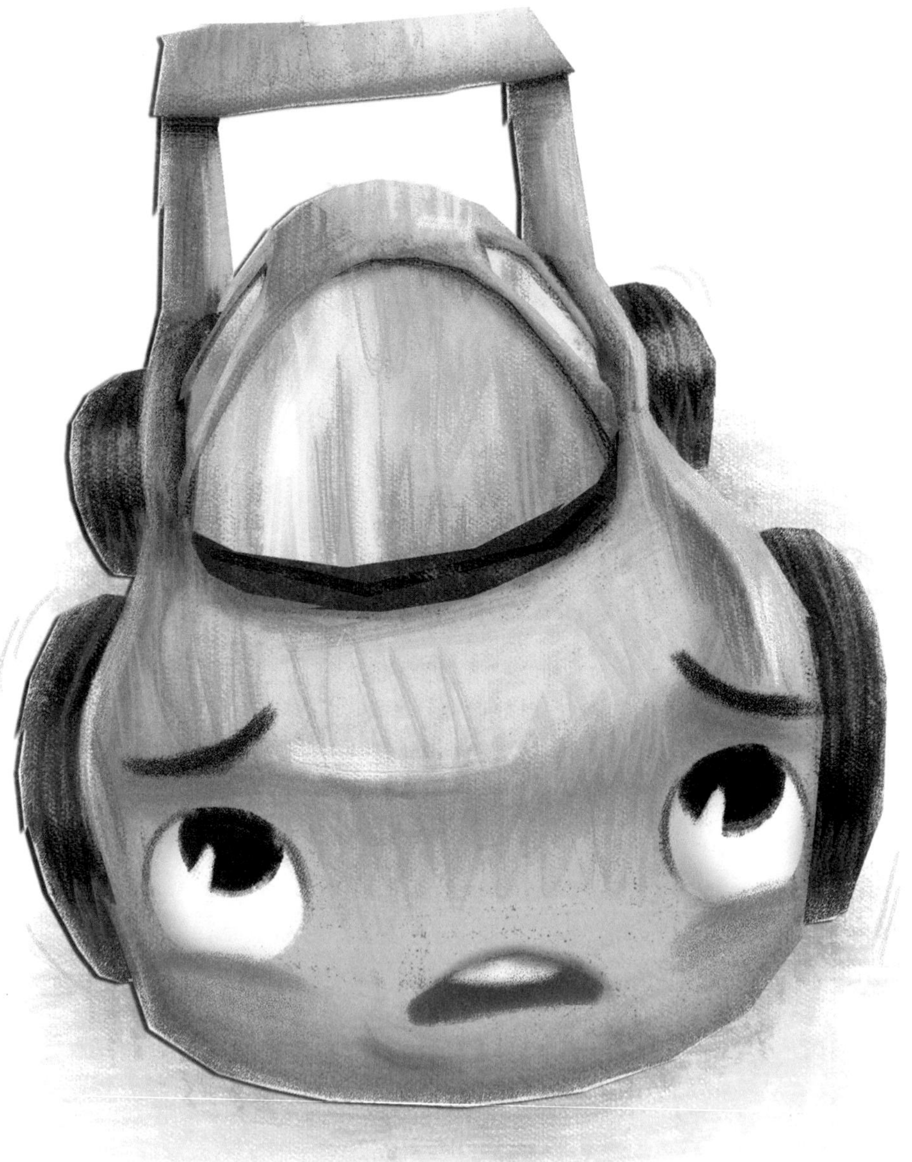

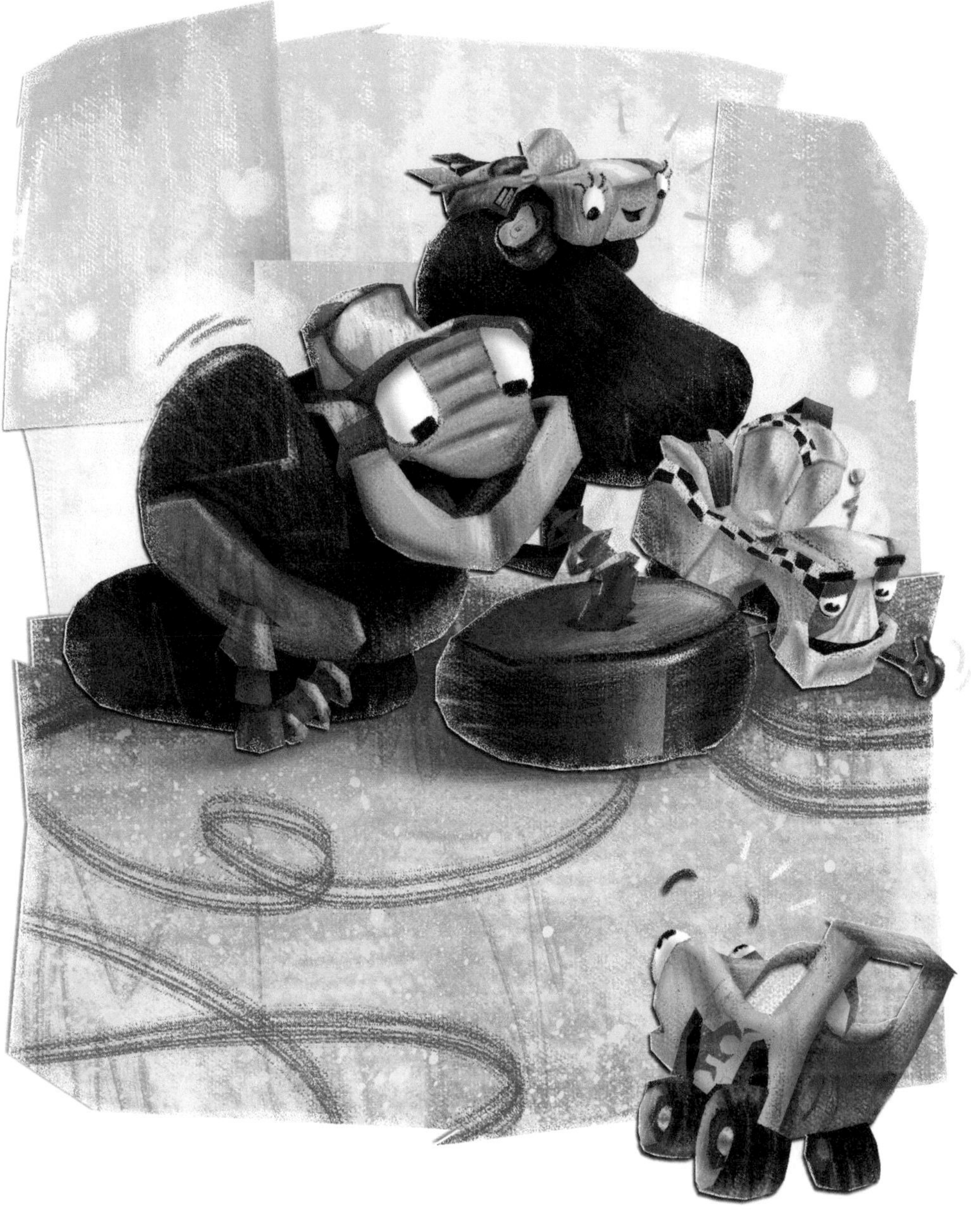

Blue stops.

Blue pulls Red.

Blue pulls Yellow.

Blue pulls Green.

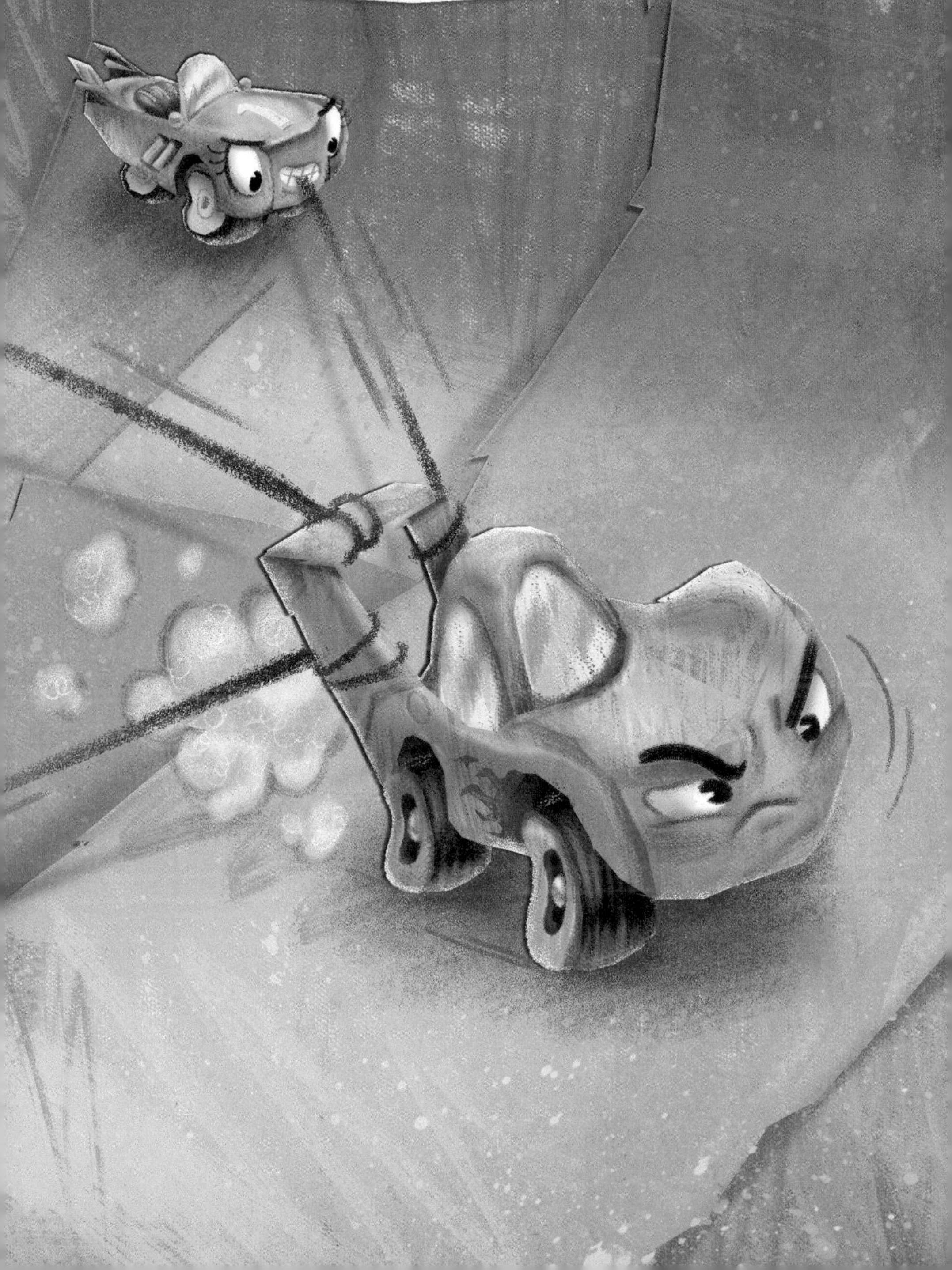

All cars grin.

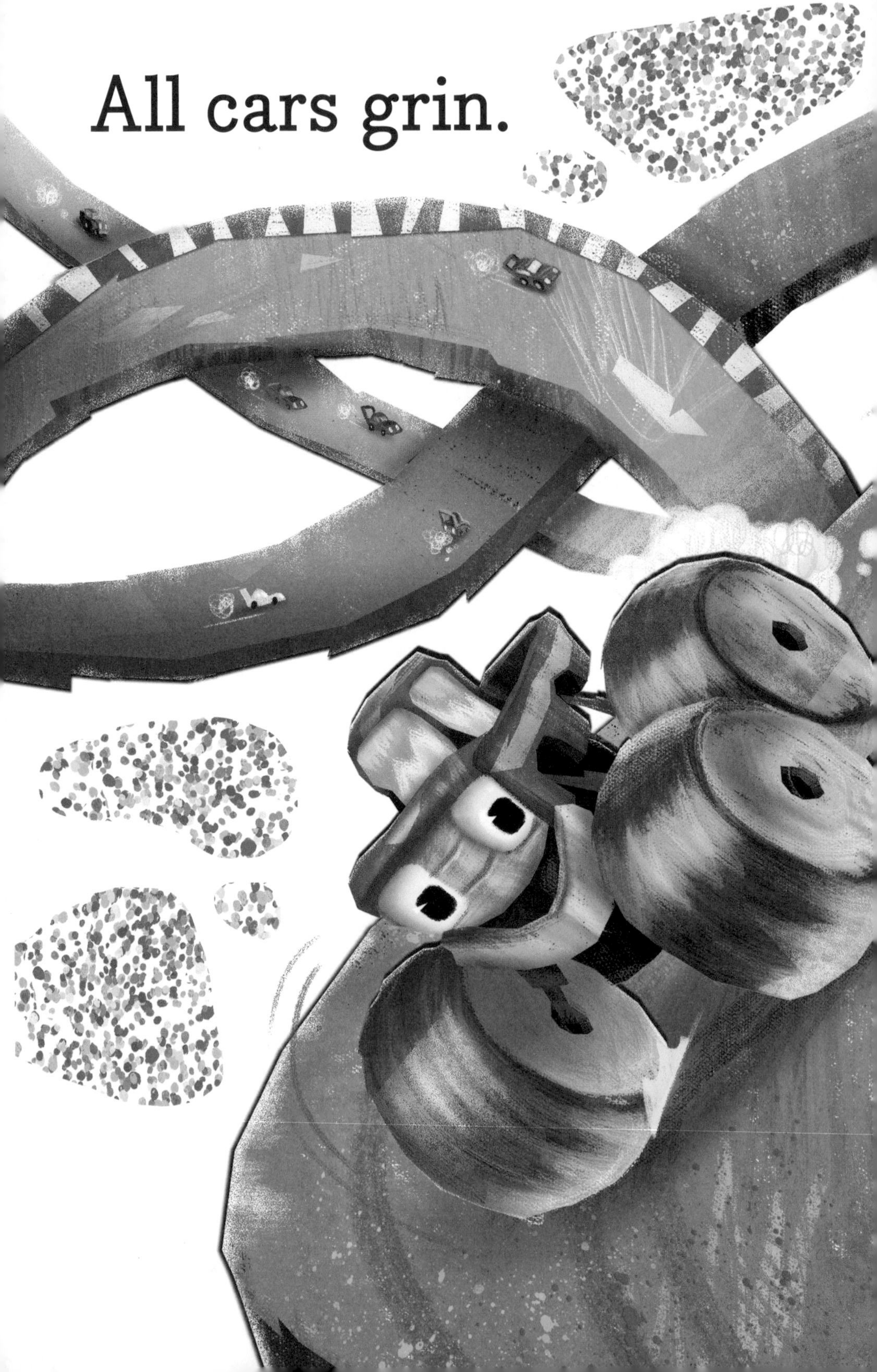

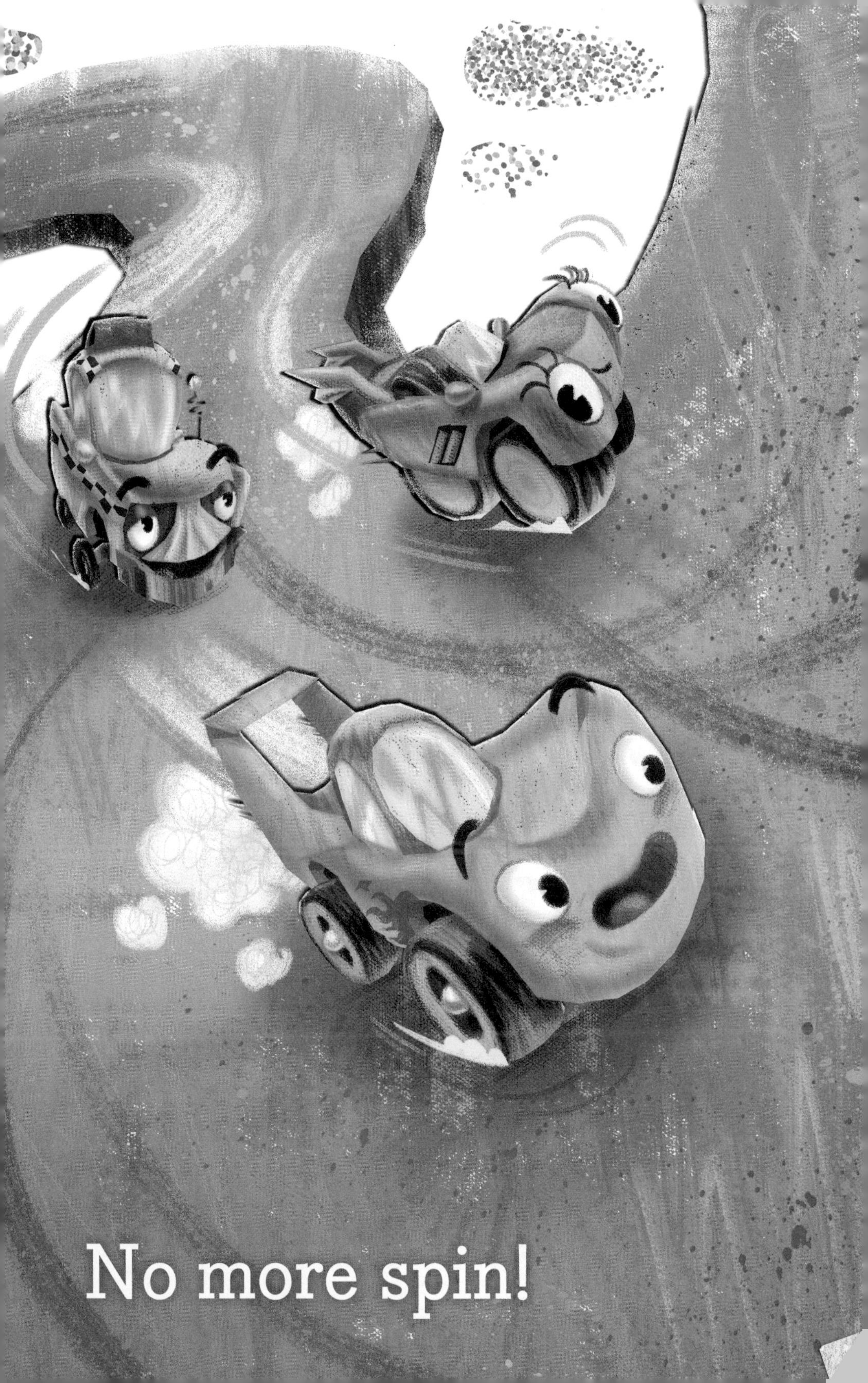

No more spin!

Zoom! Zoom!
All cars go fast!

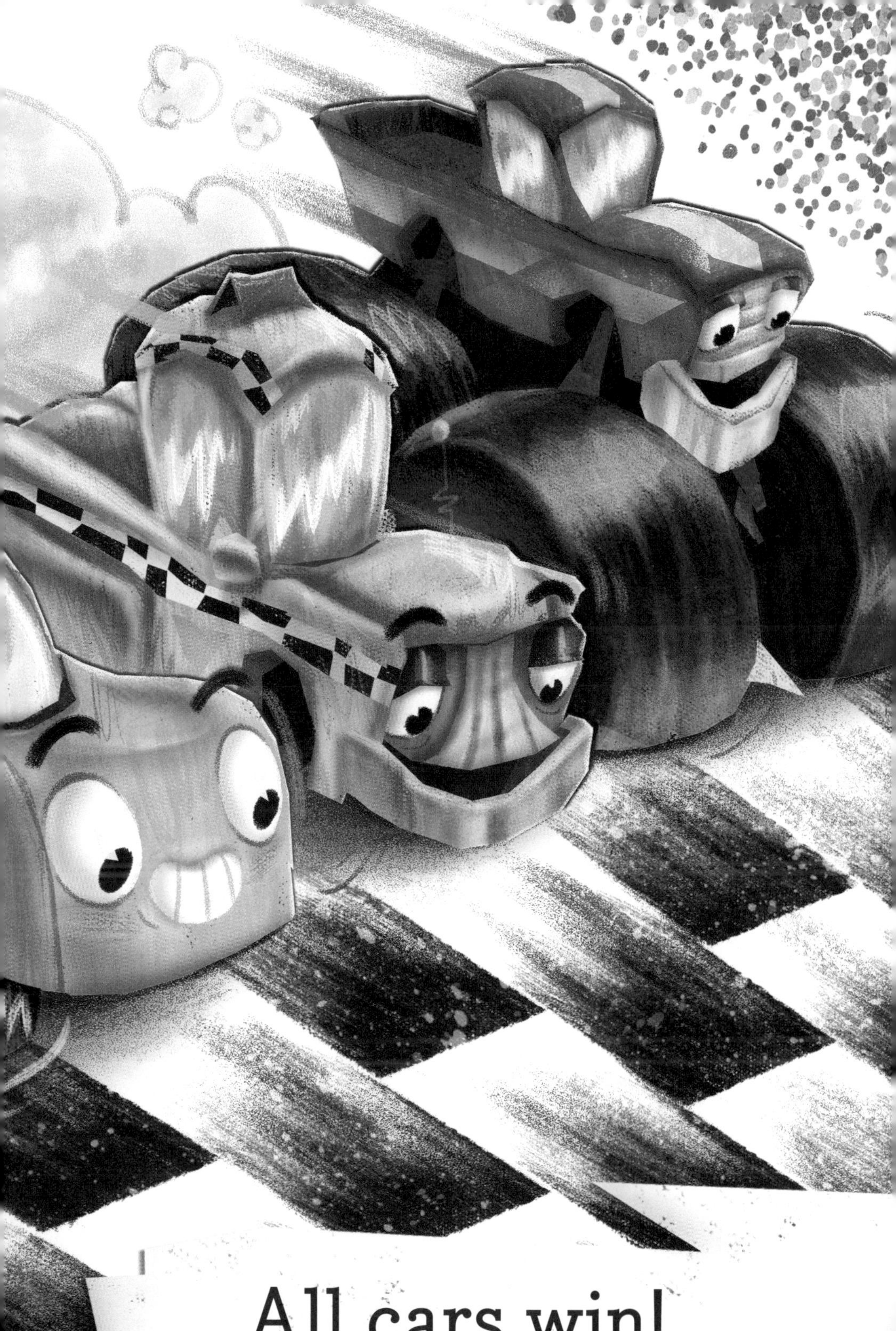

All cars win!

Now that you have read the story, can you answer these questions?

1. Who wants to race at the beginning of the story?

2. How does Blue help Red, Yellow, and Green?

3. In this story you read the words "grin" and "in" and "spin" and "win." Those words rhyme. Can you think of other words that rhyme with these words?

Great job!
You are a reading star!